This is Plop.

Plop is a baby barn owl.

He is fat and fluffy.

He has big, round eyes.

He has soft, downy feathers.

He is perfect in every way,

except for just ONE thing . . .

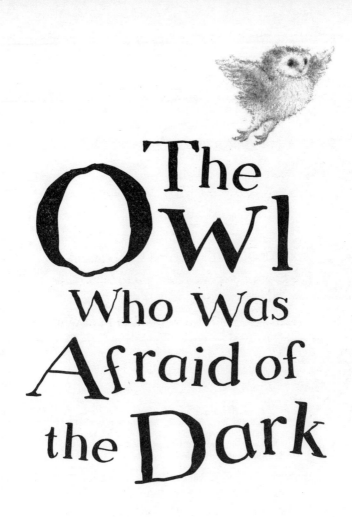

The Owl Who Was Afraid of the Dark

JILL TOMLINSON

Pictures by Paul Howard

EGMONT

For Philip and, of course, D. H.

The Owl Who Was Afraid of the Dark was first published
in Great Britain 1968 by Methuen and Co Ltd
Published in this edition 2004 by Egmont Books Limited
239 Kensington High Street, London W8 6SA

Text copyright © 1968 The Estate of Jill Tomlinson
Cover and illustrations copyright © 2004 Paul Howard

The moral rights of the author and illustrator have been asserted

ISBN 978 1 4052 1093 5

10

A CIP catalogue record for this title is available from the British Library

Printed and bound in Great Britain by the CPI Group

Contents

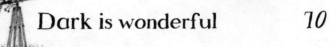

Dark is exciting

Plop was a baby barn owl, and he lived with his mummy and daddy at the top of a very tall tree in a field.

Plop was fat and fluffy.

He had a beautiful heart-shaped ruff.

He had enormous, round eyes.

He had very knackety knees.

In fact he was exactly the same as every baby barn owl that has ever been – except for one thing.

Plop was afraid of the dark.

'You *can't* be afraid of the dark,' said his mummy. 'Owls are *never* afraid of the dark.'

'This one is,' Plop said.

'But owls are *night* birds,' she said.

Plop looked down at his toes. 'I don't want to be a night bird,' he mumbled. 'I want to be a day bird.'

'You *are* what you *are*,' said Mrs Barn Owl firmly.

'Yes, I know,' agreed Plop, 'and what I are is afraid of the dark.'

'Oh dear,' said Mrs Barn Owl. It was clear that she was going to need a lot of patience. She shut her eyes and tried to think how best she could help Plop not to be afraid. Plop waited.

His mother opened her eyes again. 'Plop, you are only afraid of the dark because you don't know about it. What *do* you know about the dark?'

'It's black,' said Plop.

'Well, that's wrong for a start. It can be silver or blue or grey or lots of other colours, but almost never black. What else do you know about it?'

'I don't like it,' said Plop. 'I do not like it AT ALL.'

'That's not *knowing* something,' said his mother. 'That's *feeling* something. I don't think you know anything about the dark at all.'

'Dark is nasty,' Plop said loudly.

'You don't know that. You have never had your beak outside the nest-hole after dusk. I think you had better go down into the world and find out a lot more about the dark before you make up your mind about it.'

'Now?' said Plop.

'Now,' said his mother.

Plop climbed out of the nest-hole and wobbled along the branch outside. He peeped over the edge. The world seemed to be a very long way down.

'I'm not a very good lander,' he said. 'I might spill myself.'

'Your landing will improve with practice,' said his mother. 'Look! There's a little boy down there on the edge of the wood collecting sticks. Go and talk to him about it.'

'Now?' said Plop.

'Now,' said his mother. So Plop shut his eyes, took a deep breath, and fell off his branch.

His small white wings carried him down but, as he said, he was not a good lander. He did seven very fast somersaults past the little boy.

'Ooh!' cried the little boy. 'A giant Catherine-wheel!'

'Actually,' said the Catherine-wheel, picking himself up, 'I'm a barn owl.'

'Oh yes – so you are,' said the little boy with obvious disappointment. 'Of course, you couldn't be a firework yet. Dad says we can't have the fireworks until it gets dark. Oh, I wish it would hurry up and get dark *soon*.'

'You *want* it to get dark?' said Plop in amazement.

'Oh, YES,' said the little boy. 'DARK IS EXCITING. And tonight is specially exciting because we're going to have fireworks.'

'What are fireworks?' asked Plop.
'I don't think owls have them – not barn owls, anyway.'

'Don't you?' said the little boy. 'Oh, you poor thing. Well, there are rockets, and flying saucers, and volcanoes, and golden rain, and sparklers, and . . .'

'But what *are* they?' begged Plop. 'Do you eat them?'

'NO!' laughed the little boy. 'Daddy sets fire to their tails and they *whoosh* into the air and fill the sky with coloured stars – well, the rockets, that is. I'm allowed to hold the sparklers.'

'What about the volcanoes? And the golden rain? What do they do?'

'Oh, they sort of burst into showers of stars. The golden rain *pours* – well, like rain.'

'And the flying saucers?'

'Oh, they're super! They whizz round your head and make a sort of *wheeee* noise. I like them best.'

'I think I would like fireworks,' said Plop.

'I'm sure you would,' the little boy said. 'Look here, where do you live?'

'Up in that tree – in the top flat. There are squirrels farther down.'

'That big tree in the middle of the field? Well, you can watch our fireworks from there! That's our garden – the one with the swing. You look out as soon as it gets dark . . .'

'Does it *have* to be dark?' asked Plop.

'Of course it does! You can't see fireworks unless it's dark. Well, I must go. These sticks are for the bonfire.'

'Bonfire?' said Plop. 'What's that?'

'You'll see if you look out tonight. Goodbye!'

'Goodbye,' said Plop, bobbing up and down in a funny little bow.

He watched the boy run across the field, and then took a little run himself, spread his wings, and fluttered up to the landing branch.

He slithered along it on his tummy and dived head first into the nest-hole.

'Well?' said his mother.

'The little boy says DARK IS EXCITING.'

'And what do you think, Plop?'

'I still do not like it AT ALL,' said Plop, 'but I'm going to watch the fireworks – if you will sit by me.'

'I will sit by you,' said his mother.

'So will I,' said his father, who had just woken up. 'I like fireworks.'

So that is what they did.

When it began to get dark, Plop waddled to the mouth of the nest-hole and peered out cautiously.

'Come on, Plop! I think they're starting,' called Mr Barn Owl. He was already in position on a big branch at the very top of the tree. 'We shall see beautifully from here.'

Plop took two brave little steps out of the nest-hole.

'I'm here,' said his mother quietly. 'Come on.'

So together, wings almost touching, they flew up to join Mr Barn Owl.

They were only just in time. There were flames leaping and crackling at the end of the little boy's garden. 'That must be the bonfire!' squeaked Plop.

Hardly had Plop got his wings tucked away, when '*WHOOSH!*' – up went a rocket and spat out a shower of green stars. 'Ooooh!' said Plop, his eyes like saucers.

A fountain of dancing stars sprang up from the ground – and another and another.

Ooooh!' said Plop again.

'You sound like a Tawny owl,' said his father. 'Goodness! What's that?'

Something was whizzing about leaving bright trails of squiggles behind it and making a loud 'Wheeee!' noise.

'Oh, that's a flying saucer,' said Plop.

'Really?' his father said. 'I've never seen one of those before. You seem to know all about it. What's that fizzy one that keeps jigging up and down?'

'I expect that's my friend
with a sparkler. Oooooh! There's a me!'

'I beg your pardon?' said Plop's father.

'It's a Catherine-wheel! The little boy
thought I was a Catherine-wheel when I
landed. Oh, isn't it beautiful? And he thought
I was one!'

Mr Barn Owl watched the whirling,
sparking circles spinning round and round.

'That must have been quite a landing!'
he said.

Dark is kind

When the very last firework had faded away,
Mr Barn Owl turned to Plop.

'Well, son,' he said. 'I'm off hunting now.
Would you like to come?'

Plop looked at the darkness all around
them. It seemed even blacker after the bright
fireworks. 'Er – not this time, thank you,
Daddy. I can't see; I've got stars in my eyes.'

'I see,' said his father. 'In that case I shall

have to go by myself.' He floated off into the darkness like a great white moth.

Plop turned in distress to his mother.

'I *wanted* to go with him. I *want* to like the dark. It's just that I don't seem to be able to.'

'You will be able to, Plop. I'm quite sure about that.'

'I'm not sure,' said Plop.

'Well, I *am*,' his mother said. 'Now, come on. You'd better have your rest. You were awake half the day.'

So Plop had his midnight rest, and when he woke up, his father was back with his dinner. Plop swallowed it in one huge gulp. 'That was nice,' he said. 'What was it?'

'A mouse,' said Mr Barn Owl.

'I like mouse,' said Plop. 'What's next?'

'I have no idea,' his father said. 'It's

Mummy's turn now. You'll have to wait till she gets back.'

Plop was always hungry, and his mother and father were kept very busy bringing him food all night long. When daylight came, they were very tired and just wanted to go to sleep.

'Bedtime, Plop,' said Mrs Barn Owl.

'I don't want to go to bed,' said Plop. 'I want to be a day bird.'

'Well, *I* am a night bird,' said his mother. 'And if your father and I don't get any sleep today, *you* won't get anything to eat tonight.'

Plop did not like the sound of that at all, so he drew himself up straight and tall – well, as tall as he could – and tried to go to sleep.

He did sleep for half the morning, but then he woke up full of beans – or perhaps it was mouse – and he just could not go back to sleep again.

He jiggled up and down on the branch where his poor parents were trying to roost. He practised standing on one leg, and taking off, and landing, and other important things that a little owl has to learn to do. Then he thought he would try out his voice. He tried to make a real, grown-up barn owl noise.

'EEeek!' he screeched. 'EEEEEK!'

It sounded like the noise a cat makes if you accidentally tread upon its tail. Plop was very pleased with it.

Mrs Barn Owl was not. She half opened one bleary eye. 'Plop, dear,' she said. 'Wouldn't you like to go down into the world again and find out some more about the dark?'

'Now?' said Plop.

'Now,' said his mother.

'Don't you want to hear my screech first? It's getting jolly good.'

'I heard it,' Mrs Barn Owl said. 'Look, there's an old lady in a deckchair down there in that garden. Go and disturb – I mean, go and find out what she thinks about the dark.'

So Plop shut his eyes, took a deep breath, and fell off his branch.

He did not get his wings working in time. He fell faster and faster and finally plunged at the old lady's feet with an earth-shaking thump.

'Gracious!' cried the old lady. 'A thunderbolt!'

'A-a-a-actually, I'm a barn owl,' said the thunderbolt when he had got his breath back.

'Really?' said the old lady, peering at Plop over the top of her glasses. 'I do beg your pardon. My eyes are not as good as they used to be. How nice of you to – er – drop in.'

'Well, it wasn't nice of me, exactly,' Plop said truthfully. 'I came to ask you about something.'

'Did you?' said the old lady. 'Now what could that be, I wonder?'

'I wanted to ask you about the dark. You see, I'm a bit afraid of it, and that's rather awkward for an owl. We're supposed to be night birds.'

'That is a problem,' said the old lady. 'Have you tried carrots?'

'What?'

'Don't say "what", say "I beg your pardon" if you don't hear the first time. I said, have you tried carrots? Wonderful things, carrots.'

'I don't think owls have carrots – not barn owls, anyway.'

'Oh. A pity. I've always sworn by carrots for helping one to see in the dark.'

'I *can* see in the dark,' said Plop. 'I can see for miles and miles.'

'Now, don't boast. It is not nice for little boys to boast.' The old lady leaned forward and peered closely at Plop.

'I suppose you are a little boy? It's so difficult to tell, these days. They all look the same.'

'Yes,' said Plop. 'I'm a boy owl, and I want to go hunting with Daddy, but he always goes hunting in the dark, and I'm afraid of it.'

'How very odd,' said the old lady. 'Now, I love the dark. I expect you will when you are my age. DARK IS KIND.'

'Tell me,' Plop said.

'*Please*,' said the old lady. 'Such a little word, but it works wonders.'

'Tell me, please,' said Plop obediently.

'Well, now,' the old lady began. 'Dark is kind in all sorts of ways. Dark hides things – like shabby furniture and the hole in the carpet. It hides my wrinkles and my gnarled old hands. I can forget that I'm old in the dark.'

'I don't think owls get wrinkles,' said Plop. 'Not barn owls, anyway. They just get a bit moth-eaten looking.'

'Don't interrupt!' said the old lady. 'It is very rude to interrupt. Where was I? Yes – dark is kind when you are old. I can sit in the dark and *remember*. I remember my dear husband, and my children when they were small, and all the good times we had together. I am never lonely in the dark.'

'I haven't much to remember, yet,' said Plop. 'I'm rather new, you see.'

'Dark is quiet, too,' said the old lady, looking hard at Plop. 'Dark is restful – unlike a little owl I know.'

'Me?' said Plop.

'You,' said the old lady. 'When I was a little girl, children were seen but not heard.'

'I'm not children,' said Plop. 'I'm a barn owl.'

'Same thing,' said the old lady. 'You remind me very much of my son William when he was about four. He had the same knackety knees.'

'Are my knees knackety?' asked Plop, squinting downwards. 'I can't see them. My tummy gets in the way.'

'Very,' said the old lady, 'but I expect they'll straighten out in time. William's did. Now, I'm going indoors to have a little rest.'

Plop was surprised. 'I thought it was only owls who slept in the daytime,' he said. 'Are you a night bird, too?'

The old lady smiled. 'No, just an old bird. A very tired old bird.'

'Goodbye, then. I'll go now,' said Plop. 'Thank you for telling me about the dark.'

He fluttered up to the old lady's shoulder and nibbled her ear very gently.

The old lady was enchanted. 'An owl kiss!' she said. 'How very kind.'

Plop jumped down again and bobbed his

funny little bow.

'Such charming manners!' said the
old lady.

Then Plop took a little run, spread his
wings, and flew up to the landing branch.

'Well?' said his mother.

'The old lady says DARK IS KIND.'

'And what do you think, Plop?'

'I still do not like it AT ALL. Do you think my knees are knackety?'

'Of course,' said his mother. 'All little barn owls have knackety knees.'

'Oh, good,' said Plop. 'And what do you think the old lady said? She said children should be seen but not heard!'

Mr Barn Owl opened one sleepy eye.

'Hear! Hear!' he said.

Dark is fun

That evening when it was getting dark, Mr Barn Owl invited Plop to go hunting with him again. 'Coming, son?' he said. 'It's a lovely night.'

'Er – not this time, thank you, Daddy,' said Plop, who was sitting just outside the nest-hole. 'I'm busy.'

'You don't look busy,' Mr Barn Owl said. 'What are you doing?'

'I am busy *remembering*,' said Plop.

'I see,' said his father. 'In that case I shall have to go by myself.' He swooped off into the darkness like a great, silent jet aeroplane.

'What are you remembering, Plop?' asked his mother.

'I'm remembering what the old lady said about dark being kind. She says she is never lonely in the dark because she has so much to remember.'

'Well then,' said Mrs Barn Owl, 'this would seem to be a good moment for me to slip out and do a little hunting.'

'You're not going to leave me by myself!' said Plop.

'I shan't be very long. I'll try to bring you back something nice.'

'But I shall be lonely.'

'No, you won't. You just keep busy remembering like the old lady said.'

Plop watched his mother float off into the darkness like a white feather. The darkness seemed to come towards him and wrap itself around him.

'Dark is kind,' Plop muttered to himself. 'Dark is kind. Oh dear, what shall I remember?' He closed his eyes and tried to remember something to remember.
Fireworks! He would remember the fireworks. He had enjoyed them. The darkness had been spotted and striped and sploshed with coloured lights above the glow of the bonfire. He still had stars in his eyes when he thought of it.

Shouts – happy shouts – from under his tree brought Plop back from his remembering. He opened his eyes and peered down through the leaves. There were people running about in his field, and flames were flickering from a pile of sticks. Another bonfire! Did that mean more fireworks?

Plop watched excitedly. He could see now that the people running about were boys – quite big boys in shorts. They were collecting more wood for the fire.

Suddenly they all disappeared into the woods with squeals and yells. All but one, that is. There was one boy left, sitting on a log near the fire.

Plop forgot about being afraid of the dark. He had to know what was going on. So he shut his eyes, took a deep breath, and fell off his branch.

The ground was nearer than he expected it to be, and he landed with an enormous thud.

'Coo!' said the boy on the log.

'A roly-poly pudding!

Who threw that?'

'Nobody threw me –
I just came,' said the roly-poly
pudding, 'and actually I'm a barn owl.'

'So you are,' said the boy. 'Have you
fallen out of your nest?'

Plop drew imself up as tall as he could. 'I did not fall – I flew,' he said. 'I'm just not a very good lander, that's all. I came to see if you were going to have fireworks, as a matter of fact.'

'Fireworks?' said the boy. 'No. What made you think that?'

'Well, the bonfire,' Plop said.

'Bonfire!' said the boy. 'This is no *bonfire*! This is a camp-fire – and I'm guarding it till the others get back.'

'Where have they gone?' asked Plop.

'They've gone to play games in the dark, lucky things.'

'Do you *like* playing games in the dark?' asked Plop.

'It's super!' said the boy. 'DARK IS FUN. Even quite ordinary games like Hide-and-Seek

are fun in the dark. My favourite is the game
where one of you stands outside a "home"
with a torch in his hand, and shines
it on anything he sees or hears moving.
The rest of you have to creep past him and
"home" without being spotted. It's super!'

There was a crash, and a
yell of 'Scumbo! Got you!'
from the wood.

'There – they're playing it now. Old Scumbo always gets caught first. He's got such big feet. You have to creep like a shadow not to be caught. Oh, it *would* be my turn to guard the fire.'

'What's the fire for?' asked Plop.

'Well, we cook potatoes in it, and make cocoa, and sing round it.'

'What for?'

'What for? Because it's fun, that's why, and because Boy Scouts have always had camp-fires.'

'Is that what you are? A Boy Scout?'

'Of course, silly, or I wouldn't be here, would I? I must put some more wood on the fire.'

Plop watched the Boy Scout build up the fire. 'Could – could I be a Boy Scout, do you think?' he asked.

'I doubt it,' said the Scout. 'You're
a bit on the small side. I suppose you could
be a Cub, but you have to be eight years old.'

'I'm eight weeks,' said Plop.

'Looks as if you'll have a long wait, then,
doesn't it?' said the Scout. 'Anyway,' – he
grinned – 'you'd look jolly silly in the uniform!'

Plop looked so disappointed that the
Scout added, 'Never mind. You can stay for
the sing-song tonight.'

'Oh, can I!' cried Plop. 'That would be
soo – super!'

'You'd better go home and ask your
mother first, though.'

So Plop flew up to the nest-hole – and
found his mother waiting.

'Where have you been?' she said. She

sounded a bit cross, like all mothers when they have been worried.

'I've been talking to a Boy Scout, and he says DARK IS FUN, and he says I can stay for the camp-fire, so can I, Mummy, please?'

'Well, yes, all right,' she said.

'Oh, super!' said Plop.

So Plop was a Boy Scout for a night. He sat on his new friend's shoulder and was introduced to all the others. They made a great fuss of him and he had a wonderful time. He did not care for cocoa, but he enjoyed a small potato. His friend blew on it for him to cool it, because he knew that owls swallow their food whole, and a hot potato in the tummy would have been very uncomfortable for Plop!

The Scouts huddled round the fire and

sang and sang while the sparks danced. They sang funny songs and sad songs, long songs and short songs. Plop did not sing because he wanted to listen, but every now and then he got a bit excited and fluttered round the boys' heads crying 'Eeek! Eeeek!' and everybody laughed.

They sang until the fire had sunk to a deep, red glow and Plop had turned quite pink in its light.

Then it was time to go home, for the boys and for Plop. And when Plop had said goodbye to them all, and bowed and bowed till he ached, he spread his wings and flew up to the landing branch.

'Well?' said his mother.

'I told you. The Boy Scout says DARK IS FUN.'

'And what do you think, Plop?'

'I still do not like it AT ALL – but I think camp-fires are super! Did you bring me something special?'

'I did.'

Plop swallowed it in one gulp.

'That was nice,' he said. 'What was it?'

'A grasshopper.'

'I like grasshopper,' said Plop.'What's next?'

Dark is necessary

Plop asked 'What's next' a great many times during that night. He sat just outside the nest-hole making loud snoring noises. He was not asleep – just hungry. Owls always snore when they're hungry.

'Oh, Plop. I shall be glad when you can hunt for yourself,' said Mrs Barn Owl wearily when Plop had gulped down his seventh – or was it his eighth? – dinner.

'What's next?' asked Plop.

'Nothing,' said his mother. 'You can't possibly have room for anything else.'

'I have,' said Plop. 'My mouse place is full up, but my grasshopper place isn't.'

'That's just too bad,' said Mrs Barn Owl, stretching and settling herself down to roost.

Mr Barn Owl swooped in, clapping his wings. He dropped something at Plop's feet. Plop swallowed it in one gulp. It was deliciously slippery.

'That was nice,' he said. 'What was it?'

'A fish,' said his father.

'I like fish,' said Plop. 'What's next?'

'Bed,' said Mr Barn Owl. He kissed his wife goodnight – or good day, I suppose it was – and settled himself to roost.

Plop made a few hopeful snoring noises,

but it was clear that the feast was over. He wobbled into the nest-hole and was soon fast asleep himself.

It was well into the afternoon when he woke up. He came out on to the landing branch and looked around. His parents were still drawn up as still as carvings, but the squirrels from downstairs were chasing each other up and down the trunk, their tails flying

behind them. Plop watched
them for a bit. One of them
scuttled along the branch just below
Plop's and then stopped abruptly and
began to wash his face. He did not know
that Plop was there – after all, owls are
supposed to be asleep during the daytime.

Plop could not resist it. He bent down
through the leaves and let out his very loudest
'Eeeek!'

The squirrel jumped into the air like a

jack-in-a-box, his ears a-
quiver and his eyes like
marbles. He flashed down the
trunk and vanished into his hole.

Plop jumped up and down
with delight. But of course he
had done it again: he had woken his mother.

'Plop!'

'Yes, Mummy?'

'Go and find out some more about the
dark, please, dear.'

'Now?' said Plop.

'Now,' said his mother. 'Go and ask that
little girl what she thinks about it.'

'What little girl?'

'That little girl sitting down there – the
one with the pony-tail.'

'Little girls don't have *tails*.'

'This one does. Go on now or you'll miss her.'

So Plop shut his eyes, took a deep breath, and fell off his branch.

His landing was a little better than usual. He bounced three times and rolled gently towards the little girl's feet.

'Oh! A woolly ball!' cried the little girl.

'Actually I'm a barn owl,' said the woolly ball.

'An owl? Are you sure?' she said, putting out a grubby finger and prodding Plop's round fluffy tummy.

'Quite sure,' said Plop, backing away and drawing himself up tall.

'Well, there's no need to be huffy,' said the little girl. 'You bounced. You must expect to be mistaken for a ball if you will go bouncing about the place. I've never met an owl before. Do you say "Tu-whit-a-woo"?'

'No,' said Plop. 'That's Tawny Owls.'

'Oh, you can't be a proper owl, then,' said the little girl. '*Proper* owls say "Tu-whit-a-woo"!'

'I *am* a proper owl!' said Plop, getting very cross. 'I am a barn owl, and barn owls go *Eeeek* like that.'

'Oh, don't *do* that!' said the little girl, putting her hands over her ears.

'Well, you shouldn't have made me cross,'
said Plop. 'Anyway – *you* can't be a proper
girl.'

'*What* did you say?' said the little girl,
taking her hands off her ears.

'I said you're not a proper girl. Girls
don't have *tails*. Squirrels have tails, rabbits
have tails, mice . . .'

'This is a *pony*-tail,' said the little girl.
'It's the longest one in the class,' she added
proudly.

'But why do you want to look like a
pony?' asked Plop.

'Because – oh, because it's the fashion,'
said the little girl. 'Don't you know *anything*?'

'Not much,' agreed Plop. 'Mummy says
that that is why I'm afraid of the dark –
because I don't know anything about it. Do

you like the dark?'

The little girl looked at Plop in surprise.
'Well, of course I do,' she said. 'There has to
be dark. DARK IS NECESSARY.'

'Dark is nessessess – is whatter?'

'Necessary. We need it. We can't do
without it.'

'I could do without it,' said Plop. 'I could
do without it very nicely.'

'Father Christmas wouldn't come,' said
the little girl. 'You'll have an empty stocking
on Christmas day.'

'I don't wear stockings,' said Plop, 'and
who is Father Christmas?'

'Well, Father Christmas is a fat, jolly old
man with a white beard, and he wears a red
suit with a matching hat, and black boots.'

'Is that the fashion?' asked Plop.

'No,' said the little girl. 'It's just what he always wears in pictures of him – although I don't know how anybody knows because nobody has ever seen him.'

'What?' said Plop.

'Well, that's what I'm trying to tell you. *Father Christmas only comes in the dark.* He comes in the middle of the night, riding through the sky on a sledge pulled by reindeer.'

'Deer?' asked Plop. 'In the sky?'

'Magic deer,' said the little girl. 'Everything about Father Christmas is magic. Otherwise he couldn't possibly get round to all the children in the world in one night – or have enough toys for them all in his sack.'

'You didn't tell me about his sack.'

'He has a sack full of toys and he puts

them in the children's stockings.'

'In their stockings?' said Plop. 'With their feet in them? There can't be much room –'

'No, silly. We hang empty stockings at the ends of our beds for him to fill. I usually borrow one of Mummy's, but last year I hung up my tights.'

'And did he fill them?' breathed Plop.

'No – only one leg, but he did put a sugar mouse in the other one.'

'I'd rather have had a real mouse,' said Plop.

'So would I, really,' said the little girl. 'I wanted a white mouse, but Mummy says that if a mouse comes into the house she will leave it, and I suppose Father Christmas didn't want me to be an orphan.'

Plop was thinking. 'I don't think owls

have Father Christmas – not barn owls,
anyway – and I haven't got a stocking to
hang up.'

'Aah, what a shame,' said the little girl.
'Everybody should have Father Christmas.
It's so exciting waking up in the morning and
feeling all the bumps in your stocking and
trying to guess what is in it.'

'Oh, stop it,' wailed Plop. 'I wish he
would come to me.'

'Shut your eyes,' the little girl said. 'Go
on. Shut them and you may get a surprise.'

Plop shut his eyes tight and waited. The
little girl quickly pulled off her wellington and
took off a sock. She was wearing two pairs
because the boots were a bit big for her.

'Open your eyes!' she said to Plop, holding
up the sock while she stood on one leg and

wriggled her foot back into her wellington.

Plop opened his eyes – and then shut them again because he couldn't believe what he saw.

'Don't you want it?' said the little girl. 'I know it's a bit holey, but I don't expect Father Christmas will mind.'

'Oh, thank you,' said Plop, taking it with his beak and then holding it in his foot. 'Thank you *very* much. I'll go and hang it up at once.'

'Not yet,' laughed the little girl. 'You'll have to wait until Christmas Eve. Well, I must go now. It must be nearly tea-time. Goodbye. I do hope Father Christmas will come to you.'

'Goodbye,' said Plop, bobbing his funny little bow. 'You are very kind. You are a proper girl.'

'And you have a very nice "Eeek"!' said the little girl. 'I'm going to practise it to make my brothers jump. EEEK!' She ran off, and Plop could hear her 'eeeking' right across the field.

Plop picked up the sock in his beak, and flew up to the landing branch.

'Well?' said his mother.

'Jah lijjle yirl shays –' he began with his mouth full of sock. He put it down and tried again. 'The little girl says DARK IS NECESSARY, because of Father Christmas coming,' he said.

'And what do you think, Plop?'

'I still do not like it AT ALL – but I'm going to hang up this sock on Christmas Eve.'

And Plop took his sock and put it away very carefully in a corner of the nest-hole ready for Christmas.

Dark is fascinating

Plop, having slept nearly all day, was very lively that evening – very lively and very hungry. He kept wobbling along the branch to where his father was roosting to see if by chance he were awake and ready to go hunting.

Mr Barn Owl was drawn up tall and still. He seemed hardly to be breathing. Plop stretched up on tiptoe and tried to see into his father's face. What a strong, curved beak he had.

'Daddy, are you awake?' he said loudly. 'I'm hungry.'

Mr Barn Owl did not open his eyes, but the beak moved.

'Go away!' it said. 'I'm asleep.'

Plop went away obediently – and then realised something and went back again. 'Daddy! You can't be asleep. You spoke – I heard you.'

'You must have imagined it,' said his father, still not opening his eyes.

'You spoke,' said Plop. 'You're awake, so you can go hunting.' He butted his father's tummy with his head. 'Come on! It's getting-up time!'

Mr Barn Owl sighed and stretched.

'All right, all right, you horrible owlet. What time is it?' He looked up at the sky. 'Suffering bats! It isn't even dark yet! I could have had another half hour.' He glared at Plop. 'Dash it, I'm going to have another half hour. I will not be bullied by an addled little – little DAY BIRD. Go away! You may wake me when it is dark, and not before, d'you understand?' He suddenly leaned forward until his huge beak was level with Plop's own little carpet tack. Plop could see two of himself reflected in his father's eyes.

'Er – yes, Daddy,' he said, backing away hurriedly.

'Good,' said his father, drawing himself up to sleep again. 'Good day.'

Plop went back to the nest-hole to complain to his mother. A sleepy Mrs Barn

Owl listened sympathetically.

'Well, dear, I should go and find out some more about the world if I were you,' she said. 'Look! There's a young lady down there. Why don't you go and talk to her?'

Plop peered down through the leaves.

Standing a little way from the tree was someone wearing shiny black boots, a bright red fur coat with a matching hat, and what looked like a white beard.

'That's not a young lady!' shrieked Plop. 'That's Father Christmas!'

And he fell off his branch in such a hurry that he forgot either to shut his eyes *or* to take a deep breath.

He landed quite well, considering, but lost his balance at the last moment and toppled forward on to his face.

A gentle hand picked him up and set him right way up again.

'Oh, you poor darling,' said a sweet young voice. 'Are you all right?'

Plop looked up quickly. That voice didn't sound right.

It wasn't a white beard – it was long blond hair.

'You're not Father Christmas at all!' he said crossly. 'And I came down *specially*.'

'I'm terribly sorry,' said the young lady.

'And I'm not a darling. I'm a barn owl.'

'I tell you what,' the Father Christmas Lady said. 'May I draw a picture of you in my Nature Sketch Book? I haven't got a barn owl in it.'

'Me?' said Plop. 'You mean *really* me?'

'Yes, please. Perhaps you could pose on that low branch for me.'

Plop fluttered up to the branch and stood stiffly to attention. The Father Christmas Lady sat on a log and began to draw.

'I always carry my sketch book about with me in case I see something interesting,' she said.

The interesting barn owl drew himself up proudly like a soldier in a sentry box.

But not for long. The young lady looked

up from her drawing to find that her barn owl had completely disappeared.

'Can I see?' said a small voice down by her boot. Plop was jiggling up and down trying to see what was on the pad.

'There's not much to see, yet,' she said, 'but all right – you can look.'

Plop looked. 'I'm not bald like that!' he said indignantly.

'I haven't had time to get you properly dressed,' said the young lady.

'And you've only given me one leg.'

'I'm afraid a bald, one-legged barn owl is all there's going to be unless you keep still.'

Plop really tried very hard after that, and he only got down three or four times to see how she was getting on.

He could hardly believe his eyes when it

was finished. 'Is that really me?' he said. 'I look just like Daddy – well, almost.'

'Yes, that's really you,' she said. 'I keep one end of the book for animals and birds that come out in the daytime and the other end for night creatures. I've put you with them, of course.'

'Oh,' said Plop. 'Er – of course.'

'All the most interesting ones are your end,' the young lady went on. 'I think DARK IS FASCINATING.'

'I – er – *tell* me about it,' said Plop. (Well, it was too late now to tell her that she had got him at the wrong end of the book!)

'Hop up then,' said the young lady, holding out a finger and taking Plop on to her lap, 'and I'll show you what good company you are in. Look – here are some badgers.'

Plop looked at the big black and white animals with stripes down their noses. 'Funny faces they've got.'

'That's so they don't bump into each other in the dark,' explained the young lady. 'They can't see very well.'

She turned over the page. 'Ah! Now I think these are the most fascinating night creatures of all – bats.'

'You've got it the wrong way up,' said Plop.

The Father Christmas Lady laughed.

'No, I haven't. That's how bats like to be when they're not fluttering about – hanging upside down by their feet.'

'Go on!' said Plop.

'Yes, really. And do you know, if you were a baby bat your mother would take you with her wherever she went, clinging to her fur. You'd get lots of rides.'

'Oh, I'd like that,' Plop said.

'Yes, but when you got too big to be carried, do you know what your mother would do? She'd hang you up before she went out!'

'Hang me up?' said Plop. 'Upside down?'

'That's right. Now, let's see what else we can find.' She turned a few pages. 'Yes, here we are – oh!'

Plop was not with her.

He was rocking backwards and forwards on the low branch like one of those little wobbly men that you push. Every now and then he went a bit too far and had to waggle his wings to keep his balance.

'What are you doing?' asked the young lady.

'I'm trying to be a bat,' said Plop, 'but what I don't understand is how they begin. I can't *get* upside down.'

'Perhaps it would be easier to be a hedgehog,' said the young lady. 'When they're frightened they roll themselves into a ball, look – here's a picture of one.'

Plop hopped back on to her knee and inspected the hedgehog.

'His feathers could do with a bit of fluffing up,' he said.

'Those aren't feathers – they're prickles. Very useful they are, too. A hedgehog can jump off quite a high fence without hurting himself because he makes himself into a prickly ball and just bounces.'

'Very useful,' said Plop. 'I wish I had prickles.' He jumped off her lap and tried to roll himself into a ball.

It was very difficult. 'I don't seem to have enough bends,' he said.

Suddenly he stopped rolling about and stayed still, listening. Then he rushed back to the young lady's lap and tried to bury himself in her coat.

'What's the matter?' she said.

'THERE'S A FUNNY NOISE,' he said.
'OVER THERE.'

The young lady listened. There was a busy, rustling sound coming from the dry leaves under the big tree.

'Why, I do believe it's a hedgehog!' she said. 'Yes, here he is. Look!'

Plop peeped cautiously over the edge of her lap. A tiny pointed snout pushed its way through the leaves, and then a small round creature scuttled across the ground in front of them.

'They never bother to move about quietly,' the young lady whispered, 'because they know nobody would want to eat anything so prickly.'

'Is he sure?' said Plop. 'I'm so hungry I could eat anything!'

The hedgehog stopped dead and rolled himself into a tight little ball.

'He must have heard you,' the young lady said reproachfully. 'What a thing to say.'

'Well, it's true,' Plop said. 'I'm starving.'

'Oh, of course! You'll be going hunting with your parents now that it's getting dark, won't you? I was forgetting you're a night bird.'

The night bird looked down at his toes.

'Well, I won't keep you,' she went on, 'except – would you mind doing something for me before you go? I *would* like to hear you screech.'

Plop didn't mind at all. He stuck out his

chest and gave her the most enormous 'EEEEEEK!' he could possibly manage.

'Gorgeous!' said the young lady.

Plop bobbed his funny little bow. Then he took off and circled round, 'eeking' for all he was worth. The young lady waved, and then with one final 'eeeek!' of farewell, Plop flew up to the landing branch.

'Well?' said his mother.

'The Father Christmas Lady – you were right, it was a lady – says DARK IS FASCINATING.'

'And what do you think, Plop?'

'I still do not like it AT ALL. But what do you think? The lady drew a picture of me.'

'Well, that's very special, isn't it? Nobody has ever put me in a picture.'

'*And* she says my screech is gorgeous.'

'She does, does she? I wondered what all that noise was about.'

'Where's Daddy?'

'Out hunting.'

'Oh, jolly good. I could eat a hedgehog!'

'I wouldn't recommend it,' said his mother.

Dark is wonderful

'That was nice,' said Plop when he had gulped down what his father had brought. 'What was it?'

'A shrew,' said his father.

'I like shrew,' said Plop. 'What's next?'

'A short pause,' said Mrs Barn Owl. 'Let your poor daddy get his breath back.'

'All right,' said Plop, 'but do hurry up, Daddy. Shrews are nice, but they're not very big, are they? This one feels very lonely all by itself at the bottom of my tummy. It needs company.'

'I don't believe there is a bottom to your tummy,' said his father. 'No matter how much I put into it, it is never full. Oh well, I suppose I had better go and hunt for something else to cast into the bottomless pit.'

'That's what fathers are for,' said Plop. 'Wouldn't you like to go hunting, too, Mummy? It would be a nice change for you.'

'Thank you very much,' said Mrs Barn Owl. 'What you really mean is that you won't have to wait so long between courses! But I will certainly go if you don't mind being left.'

'Why don't you come with us?' said his father. 'Then you wouldn't have to wait at all.'

Plop looked round at the creeping

darkness. 'Er – no, thank you, Daddy,' he said. 'I have some more remembering to do.'

'Right'o,' said Mr Barn Owl. 'Ready, dear?'

Plop's parents took off together side by side, their great white wings almost touching. Plop sat outside the nest-hole and watched them drift away into the darkness until they melted into each other and then disappeared altogether. It took quite a long time, because the stars were coming out and Plop could see a long way by their light with his owl's eyes.

He remembered what his mother had said about dark never being black. It certainly was not black tonight. It was more of a misty grey, and the sky was pricked all over with tiny stars.

'Drat!' said a voice from somewhere below Plop.

Plop started
and peered down
through the leaves. There
was a man with some sort of
contraption set up in front of him, standing
there scowling up at the cloud which had
hidden the moon. What was he doing?

Plop shut his eyes, took a deep breath,
and fell off his branch.

He shot through the air like a white
streak and landed with a soft bump.

'Heavens!' cried the man. 'A shooting
star!'

'Actually, I'm a barn owl,' said the
shooting star. 'What's that thing you've
got there?'

'A telescope,' said the man. 'A barn owl,

did you say? Well, well. I thought you were a meteor. How do you do?'

'How do I do what?' asked Plop.

'Oh – you know what I mean. How are you?'

'Hungry,' said Plop. 'I thought you said I was a shooting star, not a meteor.'

'A meteor *is* a shooting star.'

'Oh,' said Plop. 'What is the television for?'

'Telescope. For looking at things like the stars and planets.'

'Ooh! Can I have a look, please?'

'Of course,' said the man, 'but it's not a very good night for it, I'm afraid. Too cloudy.'

'I don't like the dark very much,' said Plop.

'Really?' said the man. 'How very odd. You must miss such a lot. DARK IS WONDERFUL.'

'Tell me,' said Plop. 'Please.'

'I'll do better than that – I'll show you,' the man said. 'Come and put your eye – no, no! *This* end!'

Plop had jumped up, scuttled along the telescope, and was now peering backwards between his feet into the wrong end.

'I can't see anything,' he said.

'You surprise me,' said the man. 'Try this end.'

Plop wobbled back along the telescope and the man supported him on his wrist so that his eye was level with the eye-piece.

'Now can you see anything?'

'Oh yes,' said Plop. 'It makes everything come nearer, doesn't it? I can see a bright, bright star. That must be very near.'

'Yes – just fifty-four million, million miles

away, that's all.'

'Million, million –!' gasped Plop.

'Yes, that's Sirius, the Dog Star. You're quite right – it is one of the nearest.' Obviously million millions were nothing to the man with a telescope.

'Why is it called the Dog Star?' asked Plop.

'Because it belongs to Orion, the Great Hunter. Look! There he is. Can you see those three stars close together?'

Plop drew his head back from the telescope and blinked.

'Can I change eyes?' he said. 'This one's getting very tired.'

'Yes, of course. Now – see if you can find the Great Hunter.'

'He has three stars close together, did you say?'

'Yes – that's his belt.'

'And some fainter stars behind him?'

'Yes – that's his sword.'

'I've got him!' shouted Plop. 'I've got Orion the Great Hunter. Oh, I never knew stars had names. Show me some more.'

'Well, we'll see if we can find the Pole Star, shall we? Hang on – I have to swing the telescope round for that.'

Plop had a ride on the telescope, and then the man showed him how to find the Plough and the two stars pointing straight up to the Pole Star. 'That's a bright one, too, isn't it?' said Plop.

'Yes. There! Now you can find that, you need never get lost, because that star is directly over the North Pole so you'll always know where north is.'

'Is that important?' asked Plop.

'Very important,' said the man. Heavens! What was that?' An eerie, long-drawn shriek had torn the peace of the night.

'Oh dear. I expect that's my daddy,' said Plop. They looked up. A ghostly, whitish form circled above them. 'Yes, it is. I'd better let him know I'm here. Eeeeeek!'

'Oh!' said the man, jumping. 'You should warn people when you're going to do that. You know, I've often wondered what that noise was. Now I shall know it is only you or your father.'

'Or my mother,' said Plop. 'I really must go. Thank you very, very much for teaching me about the stars.' He hopped on to the telescope and bowed his funny little bow. 'Goodbye.'

'Goodbye, Master Barn Owl. Good star-gazing!'

Plop flew up to join his father and

together they landed on the landing branch.

'Well?' said Plop's mother.

'The man with the telescope says DARK IS WONDERFUL, and he called me "Master Barn Owl" and . . .'

'And what do you think, Plop?'

'I know what *I* think,' said Mr Barn Owl, not giving Plop a chance to reply. 'I think Master Barn Owl has got a bit of a cheek to send his poor parents on an absolutely urgent search for food and then not bother to be in when they get back. I thought you were supposed to be starving?'

'I *am* starving,' said Plop, 'but did you know that the Dog Star is fifty-four million, million miles away . . .'

'Do you want your dinner or don't you?' said Mr Barn Owl.

'Oh yes,' said Plop. He gobbled down what his father had brought, and he gobbled down what his mother had brought, and not only did he not ask what it was that he had just eaten, but he did not even say 'What's next?'

What he said was, 'Daddy, do you know how to find the Pole Star? Shall I show you?'

'By all means,' said Mr Barn Owl, giving his wife a slow wink. 'Anything that can take your mind off your tummy like this *must* be worth seeing!'

Plop would not rest – and so neither could Mr and Mrs Barn Owl – until he had made quite sure that they could recognise all the stars which the man with the telescope had shown him.

He was still at it at about four o'clock in the morning.

'Now are you quite sure you understand about the Pole Star?' he said to his mother, who seemed to be being a bit dense about it.

'I think so, dear,' yawned Mrs Barn Owl. 'You find the thing that looks like a plough but is actually a big bear – or is it a small bear? – and the Pole Star is – um – near the North Star.'

'The Pole Star *is* the North Star,' Plop said impatiently, 'and the two stars at the front of the Plough point to it. I don't think you're really trying. You haven't been listening.'

'Oh, we have,' said Mr Barn Owl. 'We have been listening for hours and hours. I think perhaps Mummy is just a little bit tired . . .'

'But you must know how to find the Pole Star,' said Plop, 'or you might get lost.'

'I never get lost,' said his father indignantly, 'and neither does your mother. Now be a good chap and go into the nest-hole and I'll see if I can find you something nice for your supper. You can have it in bed for once, hmm?'

'Oh, all right,' said Plop, 'but I really do feel that you should know about these things. I'll have to try to explain again tomorrow.'

Mr Barn Owl turned to his wife in horror. 'Oh, no! Not tomorrow night as well! I couldn't stand it.'

'Never mind, dear,' said Mrs Barn Owl soothingly. 'You haven't had to do nearly as much hunting as usual.'

'I'm not at all sure that all this star-gazing isn't much more wearing than filling the bottomless pit!' groaned Mr Barn Owl.

'Oh, Daddy.' Plop put his head out of the nest-hole. 'Did I tell you about Orion? Orion is the Great Hunter and – oh, he's gone!'

'Yes, dear, he must finish his hunting before it gets light,' said his mother. 'Now you get back in there and mind you wash behind your ears properly. I'm coming to inspect you in a minute.'

So Plop had his supper in bed. And then, like a real night owl, he slept right through the daylight hours.

Dark is beautiful

When Plop woke up, it was already getting dark. He came out on to the landing branch. There was an exciting frosty nip in the air.

'Now who's a day bird!' Plop shouted at the darkness. 'I am what I am!'

'What *is* he bellowing about?' said Mr Barn Owl, waking up with a start.

'I believe Plop is beginning to enjoy being an owl at last,' said Mrs Barn Owl, 'but ssh! Pretend to be asleep.'

Plop waddled up to inspect them.
They were drawn up tall. Fancy sleeping
on such a lovely night! Well, he wasn't
going to hang about waiting for them.
He might be missing something. The
man with a telescope might be back, or
some Boy Scouts, or anything. He was
going down to see.

So Plop shut his eyes, took a deep
breath, and fell off his branch.

He floated down on his little white wings and landed like a feather. Feeling very pleased with himself, he looked around.

There were two strange lamps shining from the shadows under the tree. Plop went closer, and found that the lamps were a pair of unwinking eyes, and they belonged to a big black cat. Plop waited for a minute, but what he was expecting to happen didn't.

'Aren't you going to say anything?' he said at last. 'All the others did.'

'What should I say?' drawled the cat.

'Well, what did you think I was?' said Plop. 'I've been mistaken for a Catherine-wheel, and a thunderbolt, and a woolly ball, and a darling and a shooting star, and even a roly-poly pudding. Don't I remind you of anything?'

'You look like a baby owl to me,' said the cat. Then, seeing Plop's disappointed face, he added, 'but I *did* wonder for a moment whether it was starting to snow.'

'You thought I was a snowflake?' said Plop, brightening.

'Yes, but then when you landed, I saw that you looked more like a fat little snowman,' said the cat, 'and then I knew you were a baby owl.'

'Ah, but do you know what *kind* of owl I am?' said Plop.

'No,' admitted the cat, 'I can't say I do.'

'I am a barn owl,' Plop said.

'Really?' said the cat. 'Well, I'm a house cat, I suppose. My name is Orion.'

'Orion! The Great Hunter!' breathed Plop.

'Well, thank you,' said the cat, stroking his fine whiskers with a modest paw. 'I am rather a good mouser, as a matter of fact, but I didn't know I was as famous as that.'

'Orion,' said Plop again. 'Oh, I wish I had a name like that.'

'What is your name?' asked the cat.

'Plop,' said Plop. 'Isn't it awful?'

'Oh, I don't know – it's – er – different,' the cat said kindly, 'and at least it's short. There's nothing short for Orion really, so I'm usually called "Puss", which I can't say I care for.'

'I shall call you Orion,' said Plop.

'Thank you. Look – er – Plop. I was just going hunting. Would you like to come with me?'

'Oh,' said Plop. 'I don't know. I would like to, I think, but I'm not very happy about the dark.'

'Oh dear. We'll have to do something about that,' said Orion.

'What?' said Plop. 'What can you do when you're afraid of the dark?'

'I don't believe you are afraid of the dark, really,' said Orion. 'You just think you are. DARK IS BEAUTIFUL. Take a night like this. Look around you. Isn't it beautiful?'

Plop looked. The moon had risen. Everything was bathed in its white light.

'I love moonlight,' said the cat.

'Moonlight is magic. It turns everything it touches to silver, especially on frosty nights like this. Oh, come with me, Plop, and I will show you a beautiful world of sparkling silver – the secret night-time world of cats and owls. The daytime people are asleep. It is all ours, Plop. Will you come?'

'Yes!' said Plop. 'I will. Just wait while I tell Mummy where I'm going.' He flew like an arrow up to the landing branch.

'Well?' said his mother.

'Orion says that DARK IS BEAUTIFUL,

and he has asked me to go hunting with him.
I can go, can't I, Mummy?'

'Of course, dear. But who is Orion?'

'The Great Hunter!' said Plop. 'See you
later.'

When Mr Barn Owl came in from his first
expedition, he found his wife a bit agitated.

'I think all that star-gazing has gone to
Plop's head,' she said. 'He said he was going
hunting with Orion the Great Hunter. That
was one of the stars he showed us last night,
wasn't it?'

'Well, I saw him just now with a perfectly
ordinary black cat,' said Mr Barn Owl.
'They were pussy-footing it up among the
chimney pots on those houses near the church.'

'So far from home – are you *sure* it was
Plop you saw?' said Mrs Barn Owl.

It was indeed Plop he had seen. Orion had taken him up to his roof-top world, the cat leading the way, climbing and leaping, Plop fluttering behind.

They sat together on the highest roof and looked down over the sleeping town, a black velvet cat and a little white powder puff of owl.

'Well?' said the cat.

'It is – it is – oh, I haven't the words for it,' breathed Plop. 'But you are right, Orion. I am a night bird after all. Fancy sleeping all night and missing this!'

'And this is only one sort of night,' said Orion. 'There are lots of other kinds, all beautiful. There are hot, scented summer nights; and cold windy nights when the scuffling clouds make ragged shadows across the ground; and breathless, thundery nights which are suddenly slashed with jagged white lightning; and fresh spring nights, when even the day birds can't bear to sleep; and muffled winter nights when snow blankets the ground and ices the houses and trees. Oh, the nights I have seen – and you will see, Plop, as a night bird.'

'Yes,' said Plop. 'This is my world, Orion.

I must go home.'

'What, already? We haven't done any hunting yet, and I have lots more to show you – a glass lake with the moon floating in it, and . . .'

'I must go, Orion. I want to surprise them. Thank you for – for showing me that I'm a night bird.'

He bobbed his funny little bow and the black cat solemnly bowed back. 'Goodbye, Plop,' he said, 'and many, many Good Nights!'

Plop took off, circled once, gave a final 'Eek!' of farewell, and then flew, straight and sure, back to his tree.

'Well?' said his mother.

Plop took a deep breath. 'The small boy said DARK IS EXCITING. The old lady said DARK IS KIND. The Boy Scout said DARK IS FUN. The little girl said DARK IS NECESSARY. The Father Christmas Lady said DARK IS FASCINATING. The man with the telescope said DARK IS WONDERFUL and Orion the black cat says DARK IS BEAUTIFUL.'

'And what do you think, Plop?'

Plop looked up at his mother with

twinkling eyes. 'I think,' he said. 'I think –
DARK IS SUPER! But sssh! Daddy's
coming. Don't say anything.'

Mr Barn Owl came in with a great
flapping of wings. He dropped something at
Plop's feet.

Plop swallowed it in one gulp. 'That was
nice,' he said. 'What was it?'

'A vole.'

'I like vole,' said Plop. 'What's next?'

'Why don't you come with me and find
out?' said Mr Barn Owl.

'Yes, please,' said Plop.

Mr Barn Owl blinked. 'What did you say?'

'I said "yes, please",' Plop said. 'I would
like to come hunting with you.'

'I thought you were afraid of the dark!'

'Me?' said Plop. 'Afraid of the dark!

That was a *long* time ago!'

'Well!' said his father. 'What are we waiting for? A-hunting we will go!'

'Hey, wait for me,' said Plop's mother. 'I'm coming too.'

So they took off together in the moonlight, Mr and Mrs Barn Owl on each side and Plop in the middle.

Plop – the night bird.

This is Suzy.

Suzy is a small stripy cat.

Suzy likes: living in France,
chasing butterflies and being
stroked the wrong way.

Suzy doesn't like: getting lost . . .

Read another Jill Tomlinson
and find out more.

This is Pat.

Pat is a little sea otter.

She loves asking questions.

But what happens when
no one knows the answers?

Clever Pat just has to find
things out for herself!

Read another Jill Tomlinson
and find out more.

This is Hilda.

Hilda is a small, speckled hen.

Hilda likes cornflakes, fire-engines and visiting her auntie.

But there is one thing that Hilda would like more than anything else . . .

Read another Jill Tomlinson and find out more.

This is Pongo.

Pongo is a little gorilla.

He lives in the mountains in Africa.

Pongo wants to be as brave
and clever as his dad.

He wants a big silver chest to thump!

But first he has to grow up.

Read another Jill Tomlinson
and find out more.

This is Pim.

Pim is a baby aardvark.

But what does that mean?

Pim isn't sure, so he
decides to find out . . .

Read another Jill Tomlinson
and find out more.

This is Otto.

Otto is a penguin chick.

He lives in Antarctica.

But Otto is no ordinary penguin chick. He has a very important job to do . . .

Read another Jill Tomlinson and find out more.